MIGHTY MAX

CARRIE WESTON
ILLUSTRATED BY TIM BRADFORD

D0994778

BLOOMSBURY EDUCATION

LONDON   OXFORD   NEW YORK   NEW DELHI   SYDNEY

BLOOMSBURY EDUCATION
Bloomsbury Publishing Plc
50 Bedford Square, London, WC1B 3DP, UK

BLOOMSBURY, BLOOMSBURY EDUCATION and the Diana logo are
trademarks of Bloomsbury Publishing Plc

First published in Great Britain in 2009 by A & C Black, an imprint of Bloomsbury Publishing Plc
This edition published in 2018 by Bloomsbury Publishing Plc

A catalogue record for this book is available from the British Library

ISBN: PB: 978-1-4729-5057-4; ePDF: 978-1-4729-5637-8; ePub: 978-1-4729-5636-1

2 4 6 8 10 9 7 5 3 1

Printed and bound in China by Leo Paper Products, Heshan, Guangdong

All papers used by Bloomsbury Publishing Plc are natural, recyclable products from wood grown
in well managed forests. The manufacturing processes conform to the environmental regulations of
the country of origin.

To find out more about our authors and books visit www.bloomsbury.com
and sign up for our newsletters

Chapter One

By the green, grassy banks... near the tall, tall trees... under the deep, cool water... of shimmering Blue Lake... there once lived a mighty monster called Max... and all his family.

Max had yellow eyes, huge claws, pointed ears, a big, wide mouth, sharp teeth, and a long, spiky tail.

In fact, he looked just the same as the rest of his family. Only Max was a show-off. A mighty show-off.

"Watch me!" said Max, as he did a cartwheel. His tail knocked Mum's teacup on the floor.

"Look at this!" yelled Max, as he leapt over the washing line and landed in the flowerbed.

"See what I can do!" squealed Max, as he whizzed along on his skateboard and knocked big sister Bertha flying.

Bertha was angry. "Why can't you grow up?" she said.

Mother monster looked cross. "Can't you find something quiet to do?" she said. "It really is time Max went to a proper school," sighed Father monster, looking at his flowerbed.

Poor Max. Everyone was fed up.

Chapter Two

The problem was, the monster family
stayed underwater all the time because
they didn't want to frighten people.
And all Max wanted was to have fun
and play tricks. But he had no friends
to play with. No one to play with at all.
So he was really rather lonely.

Sometimes, Max would poke his head out of the water, just to see if anyone was there.

He was mighty pleased when children dropped their ice creams and pointed…

Or when picnickers on the grassy banks screamed and ran away...

Or when dogs barked and growled and ran round in circles.

But Max's family were not so pleased.
In fact, they were not pleased at all.
"Don't keep showing off," warned
Mother monster, "or you'll get into
trouble."
"People will try and catch you,"
added Father monster, "and put
you in a show."

"You'll be fed on tinned fish and made to do tricks all day," said big sister Bertha. But Max did not listen.

Chapter Three

One day, Max had finished his sums and
read his book. Now he wanted to play.
Dad was gardening.
Mum was busy on the computer.
And Bertha said she didn't want to play
childish games.
So Max went off by himself.

Max swam in and out of the rocks...

He chased his tail...

He followed the fish at the bottom of
the lake…
"Do you want to play?" he asked,
but they just swam away.
Max sighed. It was no fun on his own.

Then he looked up at the shimmering
surface of the lake.
Max had a thought. He grinned.
Very slowly, he poked the tip of his nose
out of the water. His two yellow eyes
looked around.

Max spotted some children playing
by the edge of the lake. He moved
slowly through the water...
He got closer and closer...

He waited for them to see him.

"Look!" yelled a little girl.
"There's a monster!"

"Where?" asked
her sister.
"There!" shouted
a tall boy.

"Wow!" they all said.

Chapter Four

The children ran to the edge of the
water to get a closer look.
"What a huge mouth!" yelled
the little girl.
So Max opened it wider.

"What sharp teeth!" shouted her sister.
So Max gnashed them together.
"What an enormous tail!" said the tall
boy, clapping his hands.

Max was enjoying himself now.
He splashed and swirled in the
water to show off his spikes.

Some more children gathered on the
banks of the lake. They pointed in
amazement as the monster twisted
and turned.

Then Max did his favourite trick.
He leapt out of the water and spun
around…

Then he dived back down.
Even under the water, he could hear the
children's gasps. So he did it again…
and again… and again.

One... two... three... four... five times,
Max jumped and twisted, then dived
down into the deep, blue lake.

Afterwards, he felt a bit dizzy and
thought he had better go home.
But what a fun day it had been!

Chapter Five

The next morning, Max set off
again to the edge of the lake.
He poked his nose out and was very
pleased to see a crowd of children
waiting there eagerly.

He leapt out of the water and
splashed down hard.
The children screamed and cheered
and clapped and whooped.

25

Max was delighted. He swam on his
back with his legs in the air.
He squirted water through his nostrils.

He wiggled his ears. He thrashed his tail.
"More! More!" cried the children.

A little girl threw him a ball and he balanced it on his nose…

then threw it up in the air and caught it between his teeth. Oops! The ball burst. Max blushed. The children laughed.

From somewhere deep down, Max heard his mother calling him for lunch. He quickly dived below the water and swam home.

"Have you done any reading today?" asked Mother monster.

"Would you like some help with
your sums?" asked Father monster.
"Did you find anyone to play
with?" asked big sister Bertha
with a grin.

Max didn't want to tell lies. So he only
answered one of the questions.
"Yes, thank you, I found lots of friends
to play with."

Chapter Six

After breakfast the next day, Max slipped away again. But as he poked his nose above the water, he got a big surprise.

An enormous sign had been put up by the edge of Blue Lake.

BEWARE OF THE MONSTER

As Max raised his head, cameras and flashbulbs clicked all around him.

Max blinked.
Where were the children?
There was no one laughing or cheering or eating ice cream...

No! Max could see only grown-ups.
Grown-ups in suits with dark glasses
and stern faces… Grown-ups with
large nets and long poles… Grown-ups
coming to catch him in a motorboat!

Max dived
down and
quickly swam
to the bottom
of the lake.

By the time he got home, he was panting
so hard he could not talk. His cheeks
were red and his yellow eyes bulged.
"What's wrong with Max?" said Bertha.

Mother and Father monster came
rushing over.

"What is the matter?" they asked.

Max looked at his family. He felt very
ashamed. He told them what he'd done.

Chapter Seven

Max couldn't believe it when he saw the newspaper the following day.

Mother monster sighed and shook her head.

"Oh dear, oh dear," said Father monster.

"This is all your fault," said Bertha, pointing her finger.

Max was silent for a change. He did not feel like eating his porridge.

Mother monster rubbed her chin. "I've got an idea," she said at last. Everyone looked at her eagerly.

"In the Great Lake of the North," she said carefully, "monsters do as they please."

"Aunt Morag has a school for all the little MacMonsters there," she went on, "and Uncle Angus has the biggest garden you have ever seen."
Everyone listened in silence.

"There's a playground, a ballroom cave and lots of other monsters," she continued. "I think we should move!" Mother monster looked at Father monster. Father monster looked at Bertha. Bertha looked at Max. "Let's do it!" squealed Max eagerly.

That night, the monster family packed
their belongings and set off in the dark
(for they didn't want to frighten
people). They climbed out of
the lake...

went up the motorway...

over the hills...

and through the forest...

until finally they arrived at Aunt Morag's.

The whole MacMonster clan were delighted to see them and put on a mighty welcome party.

Chapter Eight

By the rocky edge... near the tall pine trees... under the icy water... of the deep, deep loch... there now lives a happy family of monsters.

Father monster is building a garden shed with help from Uncle Angus.

Mother monster and Aunt Morag teach sums and reading at the school.

Bertha likes to go ballroom dancing with the other monsters in the Great Rocky Cave.

And Max?
Well, when school has finished, Max and his cousins all play happily together.

Deep down in the loch, Max shows his cousins some tricks. The cousins teach Max some new ones.

Now Max isn't lonely any more, he never, ever wants to peep out of the water. But sometimes, not very often, his cousins want to show off a new trick.

They go up to the edge of the loch. Very carefully, making sure there's nobody about, they cartwheel...

and backflip... and even double twist.

So, if you are very, very quiet and wait a very, very long time, you might just see an amazing thing or two. But *please* don't tell the grown-ups!